I WANT A CAT!

Tony Ross

Jessy wanted a cat.

All her friends had pets.

Some of them had big pets and
some of them had little pets.

Jessy felt that she was the only
girl in the world with *no* pet . . .

And Jessy wanted a cat!

Her mum and dad always said, "NO!"
(Crawly, creepy, yowly things,
they called them.)

So they kept giving Jessy
toy cats instead.

But Jessy wanted a real cat.

Then . . . Jessy had a wonderful plan.
She collected lots of fluffy white cloth, some needles
and cotton, and locked herself in her room.

And she made herself a cat suit.

Next she took all of her proper clothes,
and buried them in the garden.

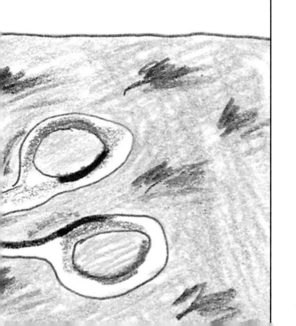

"I'm going to be the cat in
this house," she purred.

"What on earth do you think you're doing?" said Mum.

"I'm going to be like this until I get a cat!" said Jessy.
"And if I *don't* get a cat, then
I'm going to be like this for *ever*!"

On Monday, Jessy went to school.
When the teacher saw her cat suit, he shouted so
loudly, she jumped up on top of the blackboard,

and wouldn't come down, even for a saucer of milk.

On Tuesday, Jessy went to a restaurant.
"Cats don't sit at tables," said Jessy. "Even in posh places."

"Milk and trout," she said to the waiter, "and please
don't cook the trout. May it be served down here?"
"Certainly, madam," said the waiter.
Soon Jessy began to smell of fish.

When it was time for bath and bed,
Dad went to catch Jessy,
"Now you'll have to take that
silly suit off," he grinned.

"No I won't," said Jessy.
"Not until I get a cat."

Then Jessy curled up on
her bedroom floor.

In the middle of the night, Mum and
Dad were roused by a horrible noise.
It was like a million pigs falling
downstairs, and the neighbours
banging on the front door.

It was Jessy on the garden wall.

"I WANT A CAT!"

she was howling.

"Give her a cat," complained
Mr Biggs from next door.
"Give her a cat," complained Mr Figgs.
"Shouldn't be allowed,"
complained Mrs Figgs.
"Give her a cat," complained Mum.

So, early next morning, Dad went down to the pet shop, and chose a cat. He took it to Jessy's door, and knocked.

"Jessy," he called, "I've got a surprise for you."

"WOOF! WOOF!" said Jessy, "I WANT . . ."

This paperback first published in 2015 by Andersen Press Ltd.

First published in Great Britain in 1989 by Andersen Press Ltd.,

20 Vauxhall Bridge Road, London SW1V 2SA.

Published in Australia by Random House Australia Pty.,

Level 3, 100 Pacific Highway, North Sydney, NSW 2060.

Colour separated in Switzerland by Photolitho AG, Zürich.

Printed and bound in Singapore by Tien Wah Press.

10   9   8   7   6   5   4   3   2   1

British Library Cataloguing in Publication Data available.

ISBN 978 1 84270 691 6

FSC
www.fsc.org
MIX
Paper from
responsible sources
FSC® C019704